FROG GIRL

Written and Illustrated by

PAUL OWEN LEWIS

TRICYCLE PRESS

Berkeley

Text and illustrations copyright © 1997 by Paul Owen Lewis

All rights reserved.
Published in the United States by Tricycle Press,
an imprint of Random House Children's Books,
a division of Random House, Inc., New York.
www.randomhouse.com/kids

Tricycle Press and the Tricycle Press colophon are
registered trademarks of Random House, Inc.
Originally published in the United States by
Beyond Words Publishing, Hillsboro, Oregon, in 1997.

Library of Congress Catalog Card Number: 97-72345

ISBN 978-1-58246-003-1 (hardcover)
ISBN 978-1-58246-048-2 (paperback)

Printed in China

Design and composition: Rohani Design
Color: Zincografica

15 16 17 18 — 18 17 16 15

First Paperback Edition

Other Tricycle Press books by Paul Owen Lewis:
  Grasper
  Storm Boy
  Davy's Dream
  P. Bear's New Year's Party
  The Jupiter Stone

For Michelle, G.C.B.

Behind a certain village lay a lake full of frogs. The chief's youngest daughter often went there alone to listen to their songs. But today as she approached, she heard no singing. She heard human voices instead.

"Quick, let's go. We have them all," said one.

"Now we are great hunters too!" boasted the other.

When the two boys had left, she walked toward the lake, listening. At first all seemed quiet and still. Then, close by, a small voice said, "Sister, I am calling you."

"Who said that?" asked the girl, for she could see no one.

"Here. I am here."

The chief's daughter looked down to find a small frog in the tall grass.

"Oh my! How is it you use human speech?" asked the girl.

"I will show you. Follow me to the shore of the lake," said the frog.

The girl did so, and suddenly it appeared as if a low door had opened before her, but actually the edge of the lake had lifted up.

She walked under.

At once she found herself in a large deserted
village. A young woman was standing at her side.
"You see, we live as you do," she said.

"But where are the people of your village?" asked the girl.

"That is what my Grandmother wishes to ask you. That is her house behind. Come, this blanket is for you. We shall see her now."

The house was bigger and more beautiful than any she had ever seen. Inside, the floor rumbled, and it was very hot. At the back sat a small and very old

woman. She spoke, saying, "Granddaughter, I am
alone. My children have been taken, and I no longer
have their songs to comfort me."

"Do you know where my children are?" asked the old woman.

"No, Grandmother. But I have seen two boys with nets and baskets at the lake," answered the chief's daughter.

At this the old woman began to cry, "Oh! My children! Where have they taken my children?"

The fire grew hotter, and the house began to shake.

"Quick, sister," exclaimed the young woman,
"you must return to your own village. I fear
something terrible is about to happen there!"

"But how?" asked the girl.

"Close your eyes and think of the lake only. Do not think of this place."

The girl did so, and…

...there she was on the shore of the lake again. But it was no longer still and quiet as before. Black smoke filled the air and thunder roared in the distance.

Alarmed, the chief's daughter ran through the forest, back to her own village.

But there was no one there. The volcano was erupting and the forest was on fire. Her village would soon be destroyed.

The girl called into each house for anyone who might have stayed behind. No one answered—until she got to the last house at the end of the row.

But the voices weren't human. They were the voices of frogs instead—coming from a box in the corner.

"Oh! My relatives! Come, I'll take you home to your Grandmother!" cried the chief's daughter.

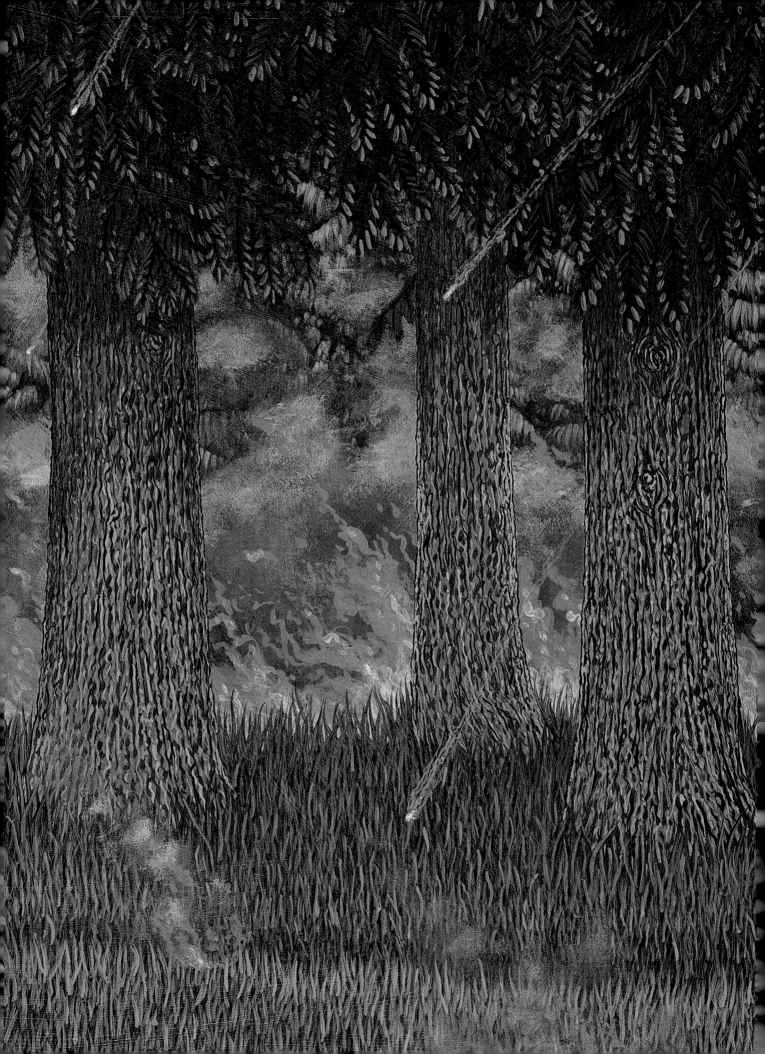

Eagerly, the frogs slipped beneath the surface of the lake.

"Farewell, my sisters and brothers.
I must look for my own family now," said the chief's daughter. "Remember me to your Grandmother!"

The girl returned to her village as a heavy rain began to fall.

Many canoes were landing on the
beach. Her people were returning now that
the rain had put out the fires.

"Father! Mother! I am here!" she
shouted as she ran to meet them.

"Daughter! Where have you been? What
has happened here?" asked the chief.

The girl told her story of the frog village, the
old woman whose house shook with fire and smoke,
and the capture of her children.

"You see," she finished, "they're our sisters
and brothers. We should treat them so."
But it was becoming difficult to hear
her. The frogs were singing again.

AUTHOR'S NOTE

Common to all the world's mythologies is the Adventure of the Hero, whose pattern of experience renowned scholar Joseph Campbell described in three rites of passage: *separation*, *initiation*, and *return*. "A hero ventures forth from the world of common day into a region of supernatural wonder: fabulous forces are there encountered and a decisive victory is won: the hero comes back from this mysterious adventure with the power to bestow boons on his fellow man."[1] In no place is this universal theme more powerfully represented than in the rich oral traditions and bold graphic art of the Haida, Tlingit, and other Native peoples of the Northwest Coast of North America.

This cosmology held that animals possessed spirits or souls identical to human beings and were therefore referred to as *people*. There were wolf people, eagle people, and frog people, just as there were human people. "Animals had their own territories, villages, houses, canoes, and chiefs, and many were capable of changing into human form at will, blurring the distinction between animals and humans even more. In their own houses they used human form, and when they wished to appear in their animal form they put on cloaks and masks and spoke their animal language. The myths frequently tell of heroes being escorted by spirit beings through cosmic doorways beyond which lie villages of people who at some stage betray the fact that they are really bear people or salmon people."[2]

Frog Girl is just such an adventure, reflecting Campbell's three rites of passage with event-motifs common to Northwest Coast lore. In it we are introduced to Volcano Woman (also sometimes known as Frog Woman), who has been described as "...the Earth Mother, and as Volcano Woman she is historian, collective memory and guardian of tribal tradition. She destroys an entire village for the failure of its people to observe the proper rituals and show respect for living creatures and cherished objects."[3]

In an effort to present a degree of authenticity in the telling, a picture-book format has been deliberately chosen in which the text or verbal content is spare and much of the culturally significant detail is communicated by the art. Therefore, for those readers interested in or unfamiliar with Northwest Coast culture and art, I offer the following outline and elaboration:

Northwest Coast motifs of
SEPARATION

• *Disrespectful or cruel behavior inviting supernatural retribution*
Two boys disrupt natural and supernatural relationships when they capture and imprison frogs from a nearby lake. Unaware, they have set powerful and destructive forces in motion—traditionally, frogs and other small creatures are protected by Volcano Woman.

• *Encountering animals who speak and act as a guide*
A single frog, who has avoided capture, summons the chief's daughter (heroes and heroines were most often of high rank) from the thieving boys' village, using human speech. The frog addresses her as "sister." This is the original indication of the supernatural relatedness of animal people and human people.

• *Mysterious entrance to the spirit world*
This concept of relatedness is illustrated further when the girl follows her guide through "a low door" to the supernatural realm, where she is told, and can see, that frogs live there in much the same manner as do her people in the natural world. As her frog companion now appears very much human, the girl—by donning a blanket bearing a frog crest—assumes an identity as a member of the frog clan, thus "blurring the distinction between animals and humans."[4]